HOPE

IS AN OPEN HEART

HOPE
IS AN OPEN HEART

by LAUREN THOMPSON

SCHOLASTIC INC.

NEW YORK   TORONTO   LONDON   AUCKLAND

SYDNEY   MEXICO CITY   NEW DELHI   HONG KONG

Hope...

Sometimes hope feels far away.

But hope is always there.

Hope

is the **warmth**

of strong arms

around you.

Hope

is sad tears flowing,

making room for joy.

Hope

is angry words bursting,

making room for

understanding.

Hope

is scared words

asking for **help**,

and finding that

help is there.

Hope

is knowing that

you are loved.

Hope

is knowing that

you love others.

Hope

is holding tight

to your mother's hand.

Hope

is your father's good-night kiss.

Hope is remembering his kisses

when he can't be there with you.

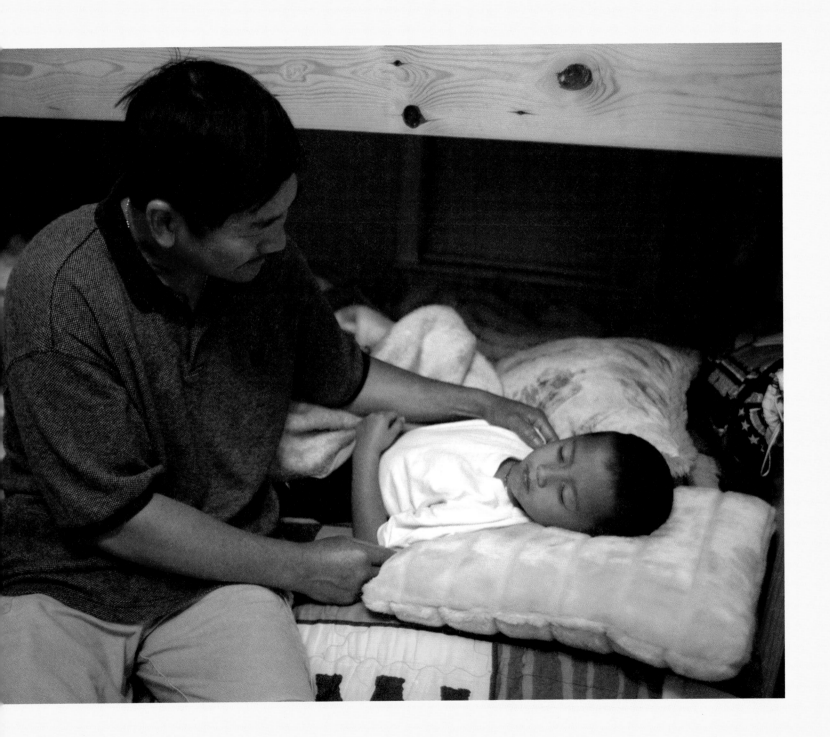

Hope

is finding

happiness

in simple

things.

Hope

is **daring** to do something

you've never done before.

Hope is remembering that you are not alone.

Many others feel

just the way you do.

Many others

care.

Hope

is a candle flame

in the darkness.

Hope

is the clear sky

above the gray clouds.

Hope is the glistening of the snow

when the storm has passed.

Hope is a heart that is open to the world around you.

Hope is knowing that things change —

and that we can help things to change for the better.

Hope

is always there

inside you,

waiting

to unfold.

More thoughts on hope . . .

Everyone needs hope in order to thrive. Hope is what helps us find the good in any situation and carry that with us into the future. I think that we are all born with a powerful sense of hope within us, along with a hunger to learn and a yearning for love. But hope needs to be nurtured to stay strong.

I learned much of what I know about hope in the aftermath of the attacks of September 11, 2001, as I helped my four-year-old son feel safe again in his city and in the world. I wanted him to know that while bad things sometimes happen, the world is nonetheless a good place to be, full of people who want to help. And I wanted him to know that it is okay to feel sad, scared, and mad about what happened. Those feelings are part of being alive, and where there is life, there is hope.

As I helped my son through that hard time, my own sense of hope rekindled as well. That experience is part of what inspired me to write this book the way I did.

Hope is contagious: Hearing the stories of how others thrive in spite of difficulties strengthens the sense of hope in all of us. Some of the photographs in this book tell those kinds of stories.

Brandy Moody and her mother, Latessa, who live in Alabama, lost all of their possessions and had to move from their home for several months due to damage  from Hurricane Katrina in 2005.

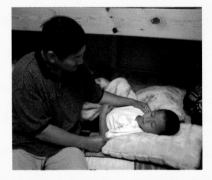 Martin Tran and his father, Ha Tran, who emigrated from Vietnam, also live in Alabama. Their house was completely destroyed during Hurricane Katrina.

With help from volunteers, the family was able to build a new home.

Jada Lavallais lives in New Orleans, where she and her family had to evacuate their home because of the devastating floods that followed Hurricane Katrina. Despite having to move  from place to place for a year, Jada remained an Honor Roll student.

These children live in Sri Lanka. Their school was washed away by the tsunami of December 2004. A year later,  they celebrated the opening of their new school building, which was built with funding from relief organizations in Germany.

 On the anxious night before a 2007 election in East Timor, a country experiencing much violence, families cultivated hope by gathering around an artwork entitled *Candle for Peace* by Jorge Pujol. The artwork was made up of 1,700 glowing candles.

In January 2010, Haiti suffered a catastrophic earthquake, and many people lost everything. Haitians of all ages came  together to share water, food, and comfort. Other nations sent airplanes and ships loaded  with emergency supplies and people eager to help out.

By keeping our hearts open, crying when we need to, giving a hug or a helping hand when we can, we nurture hope in ourselves and in others. And that makes the world a better place for us all.

— *Lauren Thompson, Brooklyn, NY*

For Alison — L.T.

Text copyright © 2008 by Lauren Thompson
Author Note pages 36–37 © 2010 by Lauren Thompson

Photo credits: Cover © Peter Cade/Stone/Getty Images. Pages 2–3 (sky), 38–39 © Jose Gil/Fotolia.com.
Pages 4 (title page), 37 (bottom right) © Win McNamee/Getty Images. Page 6 ("hope feels far away") © Mina Chapman/Corbis.
Pages 8–9 ("the warmth of strong arms") © Michael Pole/Corbis. Page 10 ("sad tears") © Corbis/Veer.
Pages 12–13 ("angry words") © U. Nölke/plainpicture/Corbis. Pages 14 ("asking for help"), 37 (top right) © Gregory Bull/AP Photo.
Pages 16–17 ("knowing you are loved") © Leland Bobbé/Corbis. Pages 18–19 ("mother's hand"), 20–21 ("goodnight kiss"),
23 ("happiness" blowing bubbles), 36 (top and bottom), 37 (top left) © Steve Liss/Polaris. Page 22 ("happiness" reading a book) © Kristy-Anne Glubish/Design Pics Inc./Alamy.
Pages 24–25 ("daring") © flashfilm/Digital Vision/Getty Images. Pages 26–27 ("you are not alone") © ThinkStock/Index Stock. Pages 28–29 ("candle flame"),
37 (bottom left) © Beawiharta Beawiharta/Reuters. Page 30 ("glistening of the snow") © John Burcham/National Geographic Image Collection.
Pages 32–33 ("a heart that is open"), 37 (middle) © Tomas Van Houtryve/Corbis.
Page 34 ("waiting to unfold") © David Deas/DK Stock/Getty Images.
Page 40 (end page) © Jo McRyan/Stone/Getty Images.

Scholastic is donating $50,000 to Save the Children's Scholastic Education Recovery Fund in connection with the publication of this book.
To learn more about Save the Children, please visit www.savethechildren.org.

ISBN 978-0-545-26888-2
10 9 8 7 6 5 4 3 2 1   10 11 12 13 14
Printed in the U.S.A.   08

This edition first printing, April 2010
The display and text were set in Minister.
Book design by Lillie Mear

*Thank you to Els Rijper for her extensive photo research for this book,
and to Karen Proctor for planting the seed.*

Every day, children face challenging situations. **SCHOLASTIC** supports organizations that share our mission to provide help and hope to children everywhere.

SAVE THE CHILDREN, a not-for-profit organization, is the leading independent organization creating lasting change in the lives of children in need in the United States and around the world. To learn more about Save the Children, visit their website at www.savethechildren.org.

LAUREN THOMPSON is the author of several *New York Times* bestselling children's books, including the much-beloved Little Quack series and the award-winning picture book *Polar Bear Night*. She is also the author of *The Apple Pie That Papa Baked* and *Ballerina Dreams: A True Story*.

She lives in Brooklyn, New York, with her husband, Robert, and their son, Owen. You can visit her website at www.laurenthompson.net.